MILK

AND

TWEETS

milk and tweets
First Published in 2017

ISBN-13: 978-1973413820

Dedicated to all those people who use twitter to make us laugh, giggle, think and smile.

And, to a special person—an anonymous person, a customer service professional—who, just before 7:00PM EST on November 2, 2017 gave the world 11 minutes of peace.

One person can make a difference!

the thinking

"A near death experience is just God butt dialing you"

#god

"Can I have 2 boxes of Sudafed?"
"Sorry, by law you can only buy one at a time."
"Ok, then just the one box of Sudafed and these 5 guns"

#priorities

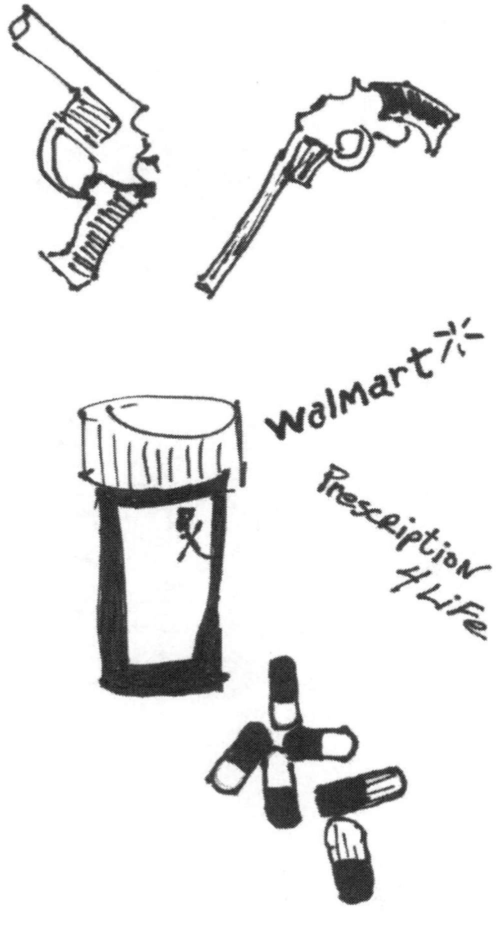

About last night…what sexual position do you call that when you cum and go?—"The Reverse Shortstop"

#promiscuous

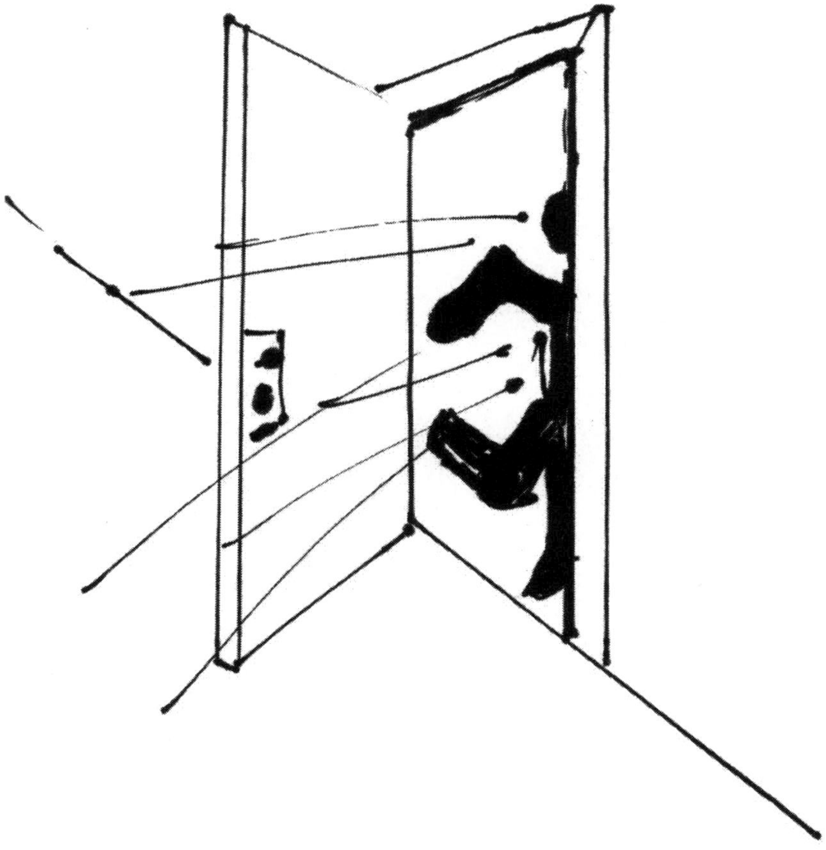

Grandpa: "I served in WWII, the Korean War and built my own house"
Me: "I'm often too tired to text people back"

#kids

Son: "Hey just saw ur text from last month"

Dad: "Funny, cause ur phone blasts rap music every time you so much as fart & is permanently attached to your hand"

#kids

"There was an *Old Lady Who Lived In A Shoe*—
and everyone criticized her bad parenting instead
of trying to get her better housing"

#america

Her: “Hey baby I’m really into 69-ing”
Me: “Oh Wow, I’d really rather 68”
Her: “What’s that—silly?”
Me: “It’s where you do me, and I owe you one”

#pansexual

Me: Siri, why am I alone?
Siri: "Opens front facing camera"

#siri

—At least she still talks to you.
She's ignored me since I told her
she had nice bits.

this is a story all about how my life got flipped-turned upside down now,

#Hollywood

Taxis driver in LA: “In my country I was a Doctor”
Me: “I get it—in Bangladesh I’m Heidi fucking-Klum”

#funny

“This Uber driver is making me nauseous…a month ago he got me pregnant”

#promiscuous

21st Century Mona Lisa: "Oh no, it's awful—DELETE IT!"

#artoftheday

Archeologist digging in a remote cave in Western Mongolia finds a wall covered in penis etchings—she texts a photo to her boss with the captions "nothings changed"

#sextou

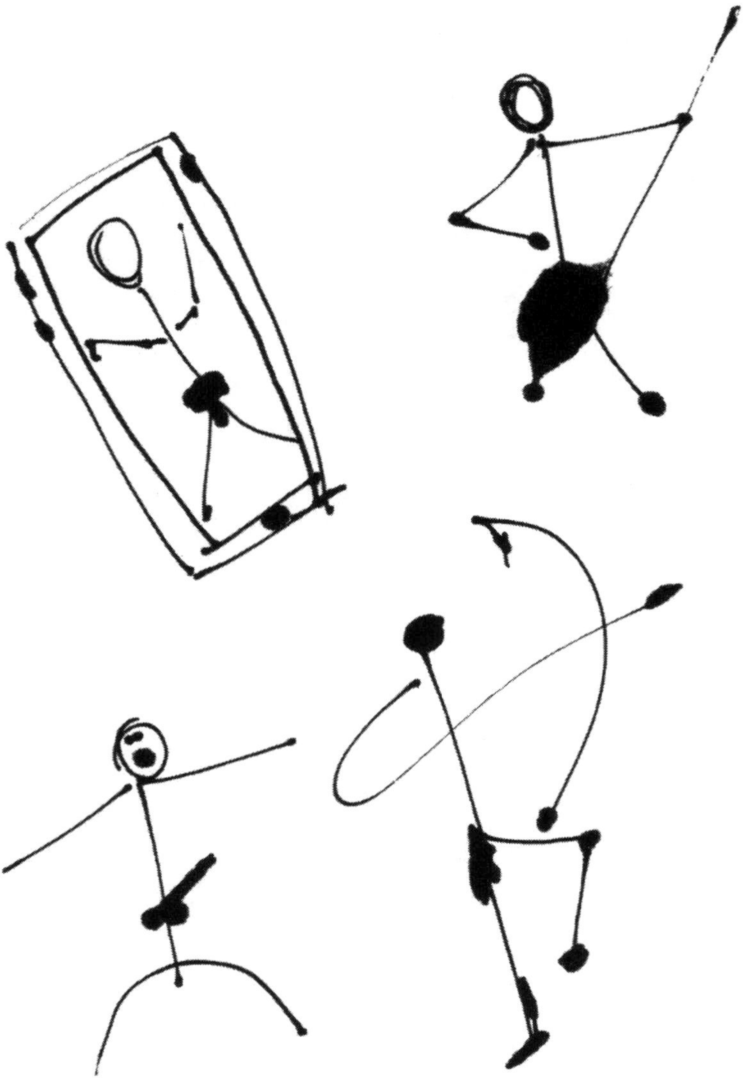

The sign language interpreter at a trump rally was just wildly swinging both middle fingers around in all directions as he speaks

#politics

—Must be speaking Republican

Pilot over the intercom: "All right folks I'd like a show of hands—which of us has ever made a small and understandable mistake?"

#funny

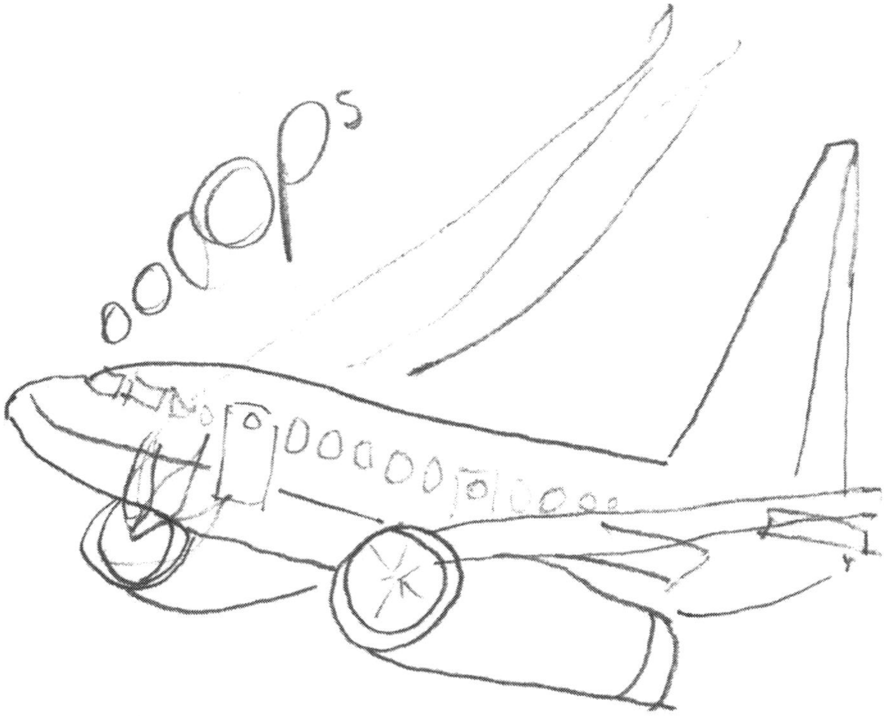

"Oh please living in ancient Greece was easy—
you point at the Moon and say look it's a
circle and you're the father of astronomy & geometry"

#history

Symptom: Wandering around IKEA with a dazed look on your face and pointing at furniture you assemble yourself.
Diagnosis: Re-Stockholm syndrome

#likealways

Saw my ex-wife at IKEA with her new boyfriend.
Well you know what they say, when
God closes a ytterdörr he opens a bildfönster

#likealways

"I once dated an Apostrophe—Way too possessive"

#dating

Welcome to sarcasm club . . . nice hair

#sarcasm

If you're a male pundit critiquing a woman's weight you should have to do it in tighty-whities in front of an audience of women three rosés deep

#wonderwoman

"What should we call this giant advertising board?"

Phil: "A Phil-board"
Bill: "I got a better idea"

#entrepreneur

If I was stuck on a desert island with
only one record, I would want it to be
the record for being able to swim the farthest.

#music

You Tube is great when you need to remind yourself
anyone can be famous but most people shouldn't be.

#youtube

I'm not an asshole, I'm just alt-nice.

#funny

the

sex

Avoid unwanted pregnancies by using the "pull out" method—this is where you pull out an acustic guitar at a party—no one will have sex with you.

#sarcasm

Wait unicorns aren't real?
are u saying I SUCKED OFF A REGULAR HORSE?

#promiscuous

Sitting in a room with my husband and kids...
Suddenly, I it dawns on me—everyone
here has been in my vagina.

#sextou

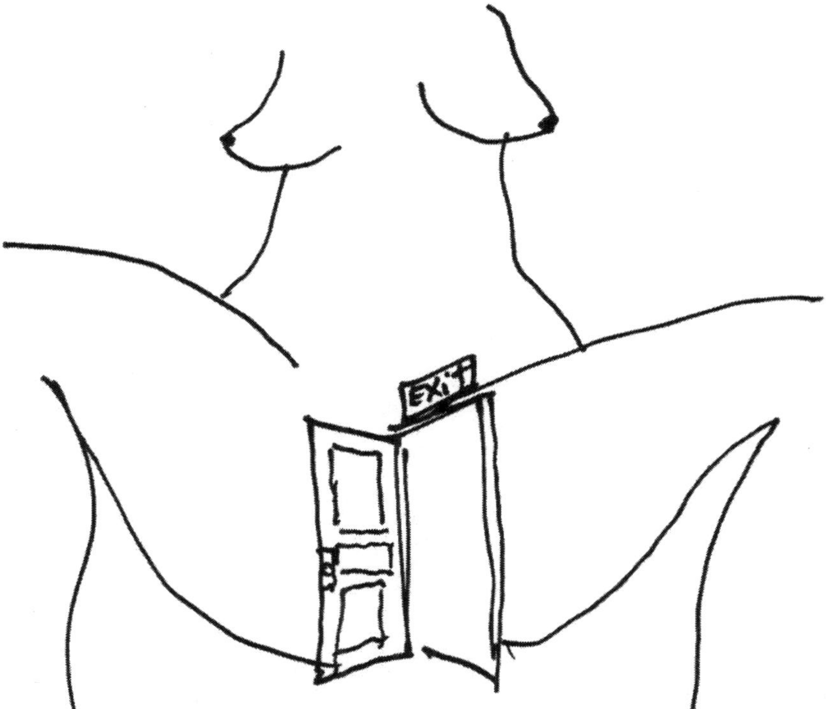

Women in 1789 opens beautifully wrapped hand-delivered packages and said, *"Oh yet another gentleman has sent me a portrait of his penis"*

#sextou

I feel like "Autumn" is just Fall's porn name

#funny

—mine's Lolly-pop Wangford

—I'm not sure you need a surname

—mine's Jack Beaverhouzen (Home of the Beaver)

Her: I like talking dirty during sex, but please stop narrating the whole thing

Me: As she complains, she begins slowly removing her bra

#funny

[having sex]

HER: "Talk dirty to me"

ME: "I've been wearing the same underwear for weeks"

HER: "No, no I mean…"

ME: "Sometimes I pick my nose and eat…

#funny

Doctor: "Are you sexually active?"
Me: "Yes, very"
Doctor: "With real people?"
Me: "Define real people?"

#funny

Me: “A pig’s orgasm lasts for 30 minutes”
Her: “So would mine, if I was having sex with someone made out of bacon”
Me: “Wouldn’t that be a boar?”
Her: “No, but you are”

#funny

I'll tell you what a woman wants.
She wants you to drag her to the bedroom,
throw her down, kiss her passionately
—then paint the house!

#funny

There is such a double standard with men and women.
When men have sex with lots of women they're
"A Players."
But when I do it, I'm "A lesbian."

#funny

Vaginas are like gyms.
I'm rarely inside one, but when I am—
I just sort of pretend to know what I'm doing
and hope no one notices—I don't.

#instamoment

—Then you go on facebook & twitter
and make sure everyone knows
you were there

I slept with this guy and left him SO speechless,
he hasn't been able to call or text since.
I STILL GOT IT!

#sexymodel

—LOL! Self-esteem is a demanding "mistress."

If I had a dollar for every time my dad questioned
my sexuality—I could afford a bad ass Harley
and probably some super cute Prada loafers

#instagay

—And maybe a pair for your boyfriend

I’m “buysexual”,
you buy me jewelry
I become very sexual”

#princess

I’m not promiscuous “per-se.”
It’s just that I don’t know what “per-se” means.
When they were teaching latin
I was blowing my math teacher.

#promiscuous

the parenting

My six-year-old boy: "Dad how do they get the hurricanes to come in alphabetical order?"

Me: "Ask your mother"

#parenting

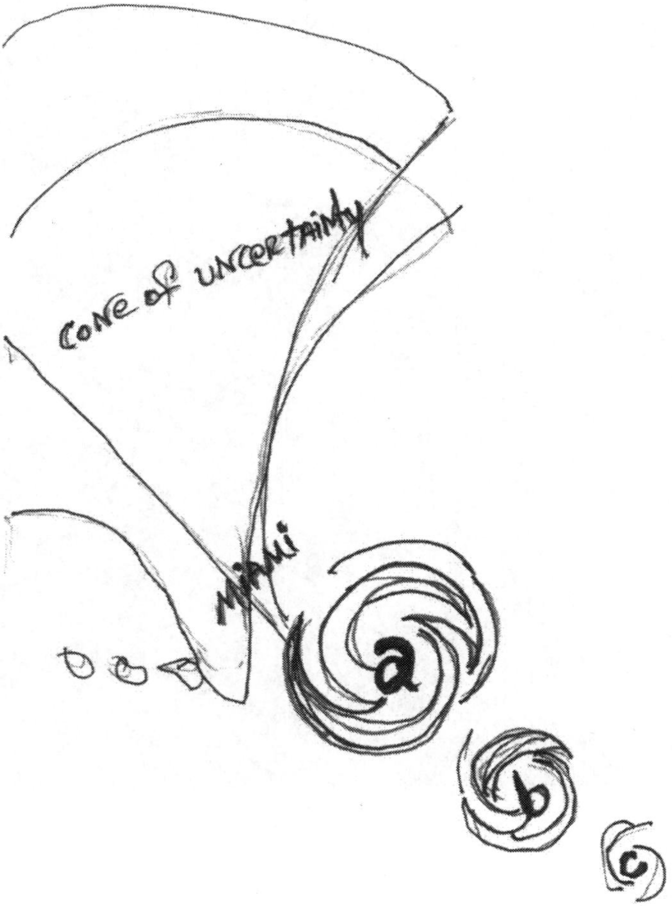

Me:	"Goodnight kids"
Kids:	"Goodnight Dad"
Me:	"Goodnight monster who eats kids who aren't in bed asleep"
Wife:	*(From under the bed in disguised voice)* "Goodnight"

#parenting

5 year-old: Dad, can I tell you a secret?
Me: Sure you can tell me anything?
5 year-old: *(grabbing my cheeks with both hands)* I just pooped and wiped my butt with my hand

#parenting

I just taught my kids about taxes—by eating a third of their ice-cream

#parenting

Me: "We already have three girls what would you like the new baby to be?"
5 year-old: "a puppy"

#parenting

Me: “It’s an old phone”
6 year-old: “Like a 4S?”
Me: “No, like a house phone that’s attached to a wall”
6 year-old: “I don’t get it—explain it to me like I’m 4”

#parenting

Day Care Worker: “I think it’s great how you let the children dress themselves.”

“It’s good for self-esteem”

Me: “Yes. . .umm they-a-they did that”

#parenting

Mom:	"I made pork"
3-yr old:	"I don't like pork!"
Mom:	"Then it's chicken for you"
3-yr old:	"Yeah! I like that kind of chicken"

#parenting

Yes we are complete now!
We used to be able to sleep in,
do whatever we wanted—in a clean house
Then we put a match to our "empty lives" and had kids
I'm SOOOOooo fulfilled

#parenting

1st kid: “My child’s snacks are organic & wholesome”
3rd Kid: “My kids eat jelly beans off the kitchen floor”
4th Kid: “There’s vitamins & minerals in dog treats right?”

#parenting

Parenthood is:
Telling you children they can’t eat brownies for breakfast
Then eating brownies for breakfast after they leave for school

#parenting

84450715R00028

Made in the USA
Columbia, SC
16 December 2017